HIS IN THE DARKNESS

ELLA JACOBS

HIS IN THE DARKNESS

http://www.ellajacobs.com

ISBN 978-87-974182-6-0

First Edition: February 2024

SHA-256 hash: eff8c6be56491aeb046e5218c
22a6ffdf56fe74f7432cefd2d3c399022fea41b

PROLOGUE

Him

I watch Sarah from across the bar. She's gorgeous as ever in her little black dress and French braids. I've been watching her for weeks, yet I still can't get enough of the sight. Even as she has her back to me, I can sense the sweet innocence rolling off her, begging to be tarnished. She turns her head to the woman beside her, and my dick stirs in my pants as she bites her bottom lip, and those pretty, big eyes light up with humor.

I've been itching to have all that delicate innocence in my hands ever since I saw her by her computer on a lunch break for the first time, biting her lip as her cheeks turned rosy. All I've wanted ever since was to tarnish and defile her. The urge only got worse when I found out about the secrets she keeps hidden in that pretty little head of hers—and on her work computer. I couldn't get my hard-on down for days.

Keeping myself in check is still a challenge

whenever I see her. For a while, I considered simply asking her out, but as I kept watching her, I became certain that Sarah is not the type of girl you court—not the type who wants to be courted, though she might not be aware of this herself. Sarah is the type of woman who needs to be taken—unmercifully and unrelentingly.

Tonight, I'll do just that, and once I'm done with her, she'll come crawling back for more.

I've been waiting for weeks now, planning and preparing, observing her closely, and waiting for the right time to strike. When an opportunity finally arose, it was almost too easy to get everything in place. I easily convinced the woman who planned this night out for the firm to pick this bar. All I had to do was put on a smile and say I knew a great place. Then I had to ask Dave, who owns this bar, to do me a small, but quite illicit favor. Being one of the few doms who comes close to matching my level of depravity, he didn't even bat an eye when I asked him. Of course, he thinks Sarah is my play partner and we're exploring CNC; I wasn't about to test his level of immorality and put my plan at risk.

The final problem was to keep Sarah from drinking—I don't like my subs drunk—which she has taken care of all on her own. The sweet, little woman is so dutiful she'll keep off the alcohol all of her own free will so she can work on a Saturday. *Such a cute little thing.* I'm almost sorry I have to spoil that dutifulness and impair her ability to think straight for a few days.

I watch as her friend slams her now empty glass onto the table and calls out, "One more round."

"Is this it?" Dave asks like he's done the last three times someone called for a new round.

"This is it," I confirm. Everyone is so drunk they won't notice something's off, let alone be able to remember, and I have a feeling Sarah won't stick around for a fifth round. I make my way back to the end of the table, close enough to watch my plan go into effect and far enough that she won't be able to recognize me.

Soon, you'll be all mine, my sweet little prey.

CHAPTER 1

"One more round," Marie exclaims as she slams her glass onto the table. She points a finger at me. "You too, Sarah."

"Sorry." I take a sip of my almost-empty Coke and hold up the glass. "I have to work tomorrow, remember?" I've told her the same thing the last three times someone called for a new round.

"Tomorrow is Saturday."

"Big presentation Monday," I remind her. I can sleep in tomorrow, at least, so I'm good to stay out late and enjoy the company, but a hangover will have my head in shambles the whole day and destroy any chance of getting some work done.

"You should learn to relax like the rest of us. You're always overly prepared." Marie gives a disapproving shake of her head, then leans over the table to call out to whoever orders the rounds. "One more round. Shots and margaritas." Casting me a disgruntled look, she adds, "And another Coke for Sarah."

"I'll make up for it next time," I promise with a huffed laugh. Drunken people really are amusing.

Or annoying, I think as Brent, the guy who works on the tenth floor and always sends me flirtatious looks, leans close and speaks in a loud, slurred voice. "Wanna join me for a smoke?"

I lean back as his alcoholic breath fans my face. "No, thank you."

He knows I don't smoke. Just like Marie knows I have to work tomorrow. *Forgetful drunks.*

With a shake of my head, I turn to Marie and Rosa's discussion about our new COO.

"Is Matthew even here tonight?" Rosa asks and adds behind her hand. "Or is he too stuck-up to join the rest of us at a regular bar?"

Marie cranes her neck to survey the two long tables full of our co-workers. "I actually think I saw him earlier. Think he was drinking scotch."

"I told you." Rosa points a finger at Marie. "He's stuck-up."

"He can't be that bad," I join in. "He's always smiling nicely whenever I see him." I haven't spoken to him since he joined the firm six weeks ago, but since he seems to fancy the coffee machine in our kitchen more than the one on the executive floor, I often run into him.

"He does have a nice smile." Marie lifts her brows in a flirtatious manner. "And his voice is like smooth velvet. Well-spoken too."

"Oh, I love me a man who knows how to use

his words." I lean over the table and wriggle my shoulders as I bite my lip.

Marie bursts out laughing. "Sure you do. But I think he's too benign for you, honey."

"What makes you say that?"

Marie quirks a brow in a you're-not-fooling-me expression. "Your desk is right next to mine. Do you really think I haven't noticed what you're doing on your lunch breaks?"

"What? What's she doing?" Rosa taps her flat hand on the table, badly wanting a piece of gossip.

My cheeks flare up as I shake my head at Marie.

She leans in and winks. "Don't worry. Your secret's safe with me."

My heart makes a double thud as relief pulls me back from the ledge of mortification. I know I shouldn't write those stories at work, but my imagination often runs wild, and I have to get it out, or I can't concentrate.

"How did that date with the lawyer go?" Marie asks, making Rosa forget about the steamy gossip.

I mouth a grateful, 'Thank you.'

The conversation turns to online dating, and I'm trying to fend off Rosa and Marie's eager attempts at convincing me to dive in when the fourth round of drinks comes. Marie immediately slams her shot down and gets to work on her margarita.

"Easy there," I say and lean to the side as a

bartender reaches in to set a glass of Coke in front of me. "Thanks." I cast a quick look up, and when I'm about to turn my attention back to Marie, my eyes catch on a man at the far end of the long table. He's holding up his glass in a salute. I look around to see if anyone else might be looking at him, but I'm the only one, so I raise my glass with a hesitant smile and watch him over the edge of the glass as we both drink. In the dim lights, I can't quite make him out. All I see is his suit, broad shoulders, and the magnetic power that seems to roll off him. He's probably one of the managers, or maybe someone from the executive floor.

Marie interrupts the strange exchange as she blurts, "Seriously Sarah, you should try online dating. You need to get laid."

My attention snaps back to her, and I forget about the man across the bar as I say, "No, seriously, I'm good." I take another large gulp of my soda. "I'll meet Mr. Right when I meet him."

Rosa and Marie launch into a long rant about the pros and cons of online dating, and I listen and laugh at their drunken reasoning for a while as I sip my Coke.

Somewhere along the way, drowsiness creeps up on me. I take out my phone to check the time and frown when I see it's only a little after ten. I guess the upcoming presentation has worn me out more than I realized. Blinking my suddenly heavy eyes, I try to dispel a wave of sleepiness before I turn to Marie.

"I think it's time to call it a night."

"Already?" Marie says with disappointment.

"Sorry." I push up from my chair and grab onto the table as a wave of dizziness makes my feet shuffle.

"Woah there." Rosa reaches out to grab my arm. "Are you okay?"

"Just a dizzy spell—happens if I get up too quickly." I lean down to hug her and stagger again as I straighten.

"Are you sure you're okay?" Marie asks, concern furrowing her brows.

"Just tired. I need some sleep." I grab my jacket and bag and give Marie a wave. I'm not about to risk a hug over the table or going all the way around it. This feels like more than a simple dizzy spell.

On unsteady legs, I make my way through the crowded bar, and a bad feeling churns in my stomach as I have to catch myself on chairs and walls repeatedly. As I realize I'm in no way fit to drive, I veer to the left, toward the restrooms. Hopefully, I just need a break from the noise and commotion, and if that doesn't help, I'll have to call a cab. Plus, I need to pee.

I find an empty stall and breathe a relieved sigh as I shut the door and plop onto the toilet seat. After I've relieved myself, I sit there for a while with my elbows on my knees and head resting in my hands, hoping the dizziness will pass.

But it doesn't. If anything, it gets worse, and when I finally lift my head, everything is a blur.

The simmering worry in my belly becomes a raging sense of anxiety as I try to get up and my legs refuse to support me. It takes three attempts before I'm on my feet, fumbling with the lock, and blinking hard to try to focus my eyes as the sharp lights hit me. No matter how much I blink, widen, and close my eyes, my sight won't clear.

Somehow, I manage to wash my hands and remain upright. Then I step out of the restroom and make my way down the short hall, back to the bar. All I can think is that I need to get back to Marie and Rosa—get some help. Flattening my hand against the wall, I move one staggered step at a time. The noise of the crowd is an assault on my senses. I pause as a wave of dizziness hits me so hard I have to swallow back a nauseous sensation at the back of my throat.

"Are you okay?" a woman says, and I blink to catch a better sight of the figure in front of me.

"I don't feel so good," I manage. "Need to..." Releasing the wall, I point toward the part of the bar where Marie and Rosa are and move a step forward. I barely make it one foot, afraid my legs will cave in if I move in more than small increments.

Someone comes up beside me and wraps an arm around my waist, and heat engulfs me as I all but collapse into a strong body. "It's time to get this one home, I see," a deep male voice says as its owner supports me against his body. I try to look up but only catch a vague glimpse of his suit. I barely even have the strength to lift my head, so I lean it against his chest instead.

"Do you know her?" the woman in front of me asks.

"We work together," the man holding me says, but I don't recognize his voice. "She tends to drink a bit too much after a stressful week. This is not the first time I'm helping her home. Isn't that so, Sarah?"

"Home," I mutter in a slurred voice. It's all I can get out and the only thing I know. *I need to get home.*

My feet move beneath me as the man starts walking, but they barely hold me up, and my head lulls against his side as he helps me through the crowded room.

"What's going on?" I manage as the chilly early spring air hits me in the face and clears my head for a brief moment.

"Shh, you're safe," the unfamiliar voice says as the man helps me into the backseat of a car and buckles my seat belt. There's a slight commotion, and then he drapes a jacket which might be my own over my legs and presses a warm hand to my cheek. "Go to sleep, pretty girl."

The car door slams shut, and it's the last thing I hear before the heavy drowsiness pulls me under.

CHAPTER 2

My body feels like a rock—unmoving, almost numb—and my head is even worse, pulsing and pounding as if heavy machinery is hidden somewhere in the thick fog that covers my mind.

It takes me a minute to realize I'm in a bed, though the faint notes of a foreign detergent and a spicy fragrance tell me it's not my own. A vague memory of a bar and my drunken co-workers flashes through the fog. I want to follow the trail, but moving through the muddled mess makes my head ache even worse.

I try to peel my eyes open, but it's like all connections between my brain and body are blocked, and forcing the message through takes several attempts.

Finally, my eyelids move, but they only seem to be twitching rather than opening because everything remains black. I try again, wincing as my head whirs from the effort. This time, I feel them opening. Still black. I groan as I blink repeatedly to clear the daze, and a dull feeling of dread turns my stomach as the blackness prevails.

What the hell happened? I feel like I was drugged. Oh my God, was my Coke spiked?

Panic speeds my heart up to a painful pounding against my ribcage. I try to move, but my body won't cooperate. All I manage is a slight movement against the mattress that makes me realize I'm naked under the comforter.

Oh God, oh God, oh God. Where the hell am I? Why am I naked?

My breaths become erratic puffs of air, and my chest aches with the effort as I try to drag the air deep into my lungs but only manage shallow gulps.

I blink my eyes wildly and finally manage to move my head toward a dim source of light to my left, but I move too quickly, causing a sharp spear of pain to slash through my head. Squeezing my eyes shut, I groan and clench my jaw until I don't feel like my head is about to burst anymore. Then I peel my eyes open and blink wildly toward a soft sphere of light. Letting my eyes roam a bit, I find a vague shadow close to the light, like the blurry outlines of an armchair along with minuscule movement as if someone is occupying said chair.

"Whe–" I swallow against the dryness in my throat and try again. "Where am I?" My voice comes out shrill and thin as panic pulses through my system. I blink again and everything remains shrouded in a cloak of darkness as if I'm seeing it all from under a blanket—but there's no fabric over my eyes. "Why can't I see?"

I keep blinking, ignoring the thrumming ache in my head. Still nothing but the vague light and outlines. Once again, I try to move, but my head is too dull to listen, my body too numb to react. The panic remains trapped inside my mind, and claustrophobia seeps in, pulsing in my listless libs and squeezing my lungs.

"Black contacts," a male voice explains.

I yelp at the sound and once again whip my head to my left—toward the chair—and groan. "What?" I croak as I go deadly still. I wait for more, but all I hear are my heavy breaths billowing into the room, loud and agitated. No additional words. But the echo of that deep, steady voice remains in my inner ear—the slightly rough edge that has me shuddering.

There's a soft creak and the slight shuffle of feet against the floor, like the man is getting up from a chair.

A shadow moves before me, and my heart feels like it's about to give in when the mattress dips. The brush of fingers on my skin makes me jerk. My body finally reacts as I try to pull out of the stranger's reach, but he simply snatches my arm.

"What—why—" I stutter as I try to come up with something to say, but my head remains stuck in panicked claustrophobia, unable to pull anything sensible out of the haze. "Please don't hurt me," I end up saying in a voice so weak I barely recognize it.

His fingers slowly slide off my arm, and the mattress dips beside my head as if bearing the weight of his hand as he leans close. A hot breath fans my cheeks, bringing me the scent of a spicy cologne and something woodsy, like a rich scotch.

He brushes my hair from my forehead, and I get an eerie sense of way too much control as he speaks. "Don't overwork your head with too many questions. It must be aching enough as it is." He trails his fingers along my cheek and down my neck, eliciting a shuddery sensation that raises goosebumps in its wake. He continues down to my chest, where he flattens his hand below my throat in a soothing gesture. For a moment, it works. My breathing steadies beneath his warm touch, and my spinning mind comes to a halt.

But then he speaks.

"All you need to know is that you're mine for the night. You'll submit your body and your mind to me as long as the darkness bears heavy over the city, and in return, I'll give you your sight back and let you leave come morning."

"No," I whimper as I try to push to the side in a frantic attempt to get away. I have no idea who this man is. Nothing about his voice rings familiar.

"Shh-sh-shh." He grabs both my arms, gently this time, and holds me still. "There's nothing you can do about it," he says like it's supposed to reassure me. "Your hands are trapped, your eyes are blind, and a chain connects your collar to the bedpost." He releases my arm to reach for something near my head, and a small tug at my throat pulls my awareness to the devastating feeling of metal encircling my neck.

How could I not have noticed? What kind of drug has he given me to make me this disoriented?

When I lift a hand to touch the collar, I realize what he meant by my hands being trapped. My hand is stuck in a fist—encased in a thick material that feels like leather. Lifting my other hand, I find it stuck too, and humiliation washes through me as I try to open my hands without luck. I strain my fingers against the confining material and move my hands against the collar, but all I manage is to press against the solid band to feel the steel dig deeper into my skin. Even if the collar isn't locked, there's no way for me to get it off.

The man gently nudges my hand back down. "Don't waste your energy. Everything is locked. The mittens too. No use in destroying your teeth trying to bite them off."

"What do you want from me?" I manage in a weak voice as the realization sinks into my hazy brain: I'm trapped, well and good, completely at this man's mercy.

"First, I'll let you rest for a bit. Let the drugs clear out of your system." He gently scoots a hand under my back and gives me a push. "Come, sit up."

My body is so dull and disconnected from my brain that I can barely lift my chest, and I have to rely on his strength to help me up. The movement seems to clear some of the numbness from my body, and as he helps me up to sit against the headboard, I go from feeling nothing to feeling way too much. My head is pounding like the shrill sound of a drill going at a staccato pace, and my entire body is so weak and useless that shivers spread through my muscles from the sheer effort of sitting up. Or maybe it's the shock that has finally seeped into my limbs. Or it's the slight chill in the room as the air fans my naked skin.

I want to fight or at least plead with him, but I don't have the strength. Powerlessness is a tightening vise around my chest, and all I can do is wrap my arms around myself in an attempt to alleviate the chill. The touch of leather on my arms only solidifies my helplessness, and tears pool in my eyes.

My captor pulls a comforter around my body and tucks it in place, but the heat offers no relief. The shaking only intensifies as the fog in my mind draws back, clearing the way for the shock and horror of it all to sink deeper, devastating and defeating.

"Please," I say as I move my head and blink like it could somehow bring back my sight.

"Open your mouth. A couple of aspirin will help with the headache." He presses his thumb to my lower lip, coaxing it open so he can place two pills on my tongue. Then he holds a glass of water to my lips, and I obediently drink and swallow, not knowing what else to do. I have no idea whether the pills that are now in my system are actually aspirin, but the pounding ache in my head is too loud, the weight of my situation too heavy to consider what else it could be.

"Here, drink some more." He cups the back of my head as he holds the glass to my lips again. Once the glass is empty, he removes it and prods a piece of fruit at my lips.

"Eat, you'll need the energy," he simply says, and then the room descends into silence as he feeds me pieces of sweet pineapple, mango, and strawberries.

There's no telling how much time passes like this. I remain as still as I can to subdue the ache in my head.

I realize I must have zoned out for a while when he speaks again, because the sharp sensations in my head are gone and the shaking in my body has settled. I still feel weak and heavy, but not in the same crushing way as before, and when he helps me to lie back down, I can move a bit more on my own.

"I'll be right back," he says, giving me a reassuring squeeze on the arm. The mattress moves as he gets up, and his footsteps resound through the room before the sound of a door opening and closing leaves me in dead silence.

I blink toward my surroundings, trying to catch sight of something—anything—through the contact lenses. All I see is the dim light beside the bed and the vague outline of the tall armchair. When I turn my head to the other side or squint to see further into the room, it's all black. My chest tightens under the weight of it all, but I refuse to let it fester, so I move my attention on to investigate the next thing. I need to get a better sense of my predicament.

Keeping my hands in front of me to make sure I won't suddenly fall over the edge, I move in increments across the bed to test my range of movement. My hands have just found the edge of the mattress when my neck catches on the chain and metal digs into my neck. I swallow hard and push down the crushing feeling that threatens to pull me under, then turn and move to the other side until the chain stops me. I ascertain I have plenty of space to move around, yet not enough to leave the bed. I'm not sure what to do with this information. I'm sort of grateful he's made sure I won't fall out of bed in my blind helplessness, but the size of the bed is intimidating. It's larger than any regular bed I've ever slept in, and when I move a little on the mattress, I realize it's extremely comfortable, and so are the sheets.

Realizing my captor may be rich makes me shudder. It means he has the resources to effectively lock me in place and put me at his mercy. And more so, I sensed this sort of calculated control within him, and the combination is scarier than the loss of my sight and touch combined.

CHAPTER 3

My entire system is on high alert when he returns. I look for more light and listen for sounds, anything to give me some idea of where I am or who this man is. All I see is a vague shadow as he moves through the room and takes a seat in the armchair to my left, and the only sounds I hear are his firm steps and rustling paper.

"I want to read you a story, Sarah," he says. "Can you be a good girl and listen attentively?"

I frown in confusion. I thought he was going to use my body, and now he wants to read to me? Is it some kind of twisted game, or is he more of a lunatic than I had initially thought?

"Can you?" he repeats with more edge.

"Yes." I swallow and wet my lips. "Of course."

"Good girl," he croons, and the sweet appraisal has a strange effect on me that I don't dare to acknowledge.

I shift a bit on the mattress to get comfortable. Or maybe it's to quell the tingling swirl of warmth in my belly.

"Rain was pelting against the window shield as I drove through town," he reads. "The rain was so heavy the wipers could barely keep up, and I had to squint to make out the road as streetlights blended with the water in blurry visions. A car behind me honked, and I realized it's because the light was green."

Something sounds familiar about the words, but I can't quite put my finger on it. All I know is that the foreboding atmosphere goes perfectly well with the feeling in my gut.

He continues reading. "I breathed a sigh of relief as I pulled up at the bar where I was going to meet my co-workers for Friday night drinks. *Now, that felt like a close brush with death.* The first thing I noticed when I entered the bar and approached our table was the new man beside Clarice. A man with black hair, gray at the temples, and eyes like blue diamonds that watched me like—"

"No, stop!" I erupt, realizing it's my own words. *My* story. "How did you get that? I don't want to hear it!" I'm so desperate not to hear more that I'm almost of the mind to press the mittens to my ears and say 'La, la, la, la, la.'

But it's the harsh sound of a "Shh," cutting through the air that halts my outbreak. His low voice rumbles with a subtle sort of menace as he says, "Quit acting like a child and own up to your desires."

"I don't want to hear it," I repeat, now more meekly.

"You're going to hear it whether you want to or not. I'd rather wait until you've calmed down, but if you keep complaining, I'll have to stuff your mouth."

The threat hangs thick in the air as I bite my lips, not daring to provoke him and test whether he's bluffing. Because I know he isn't.

"Much better." Paper rustles, and he keeps reading, laying all my filthy fantasies out there in the open. I'm almost grateful I can't see as he speaks words that were never meant to be said out loud—dirty desires about dominance and submission, pleasure and pain, and even humiliation.

When he's read the last line, he lets me hover in silent mortification for a minute before he speaks again.

"Which was your favorite part, Sarah?" He moves to sit on the bed, and when I only shake my head, he adds, "Was it the kidnapping? Maybe the dingy basement? Or the way he came on her face then scooped it into her mouth?"

I still don't answer. My throat is too tight with knots to say anything even if I wanted to.

"Do you want to know my favorite part?" He trails a finger down between my breasts with a touch so light that tingling sensations erupt beneath it. Then he moves back up to linger at the hollow of my throat, teasing with the tip of his finger. "Can you guess it?"

My breath speeds up, but I'm not sure if it's from fear or the titillating promise of more to come—his finger touching that exact spot I often dream a man would touch. I've never dared to ask any of my previous boyfriends to do it, but the desire has always been there—for them to wrap a hand around my neck and tighten until my airways narrow and I can feel the rush of the power exchange.

"No," I say in a breathy voice.

He hums as he slides his fingers down the sides of my throat, pushing the collar up as he settles his palm over my windpipe. "I loved the part where he takes her breath." He tightens his fingers around my neck in a snug grip, and my whole system buzzes with a potent mix of fear and anticipation as he starts squeezing.

"Please don't," I say in a weak voice.

"The hand on the throat part was delicious." He squeezes a bit tighter, just enough for me to feel the pressure in my windpipe. "But what really got me hard was when he shoved a dildo down her throat. I was supposed to go to a meeting after I read that, but I had to stay in my office for half an hour because I couldn't get my erection down." He gives me a slight shake by the throat that pulls a whimper from me. "I should punish you for making me late, but we'll save that for later."

Lifting his other hand to my face, he presses his finger to my bottom lip. I'm so caught in the fear, or maybe the heady trance, that I open to let him in. He slides the digit over my tongue as he speaks.

"Knowing the pretty, little innocent-looking girl on the ninth floor had come up with such a filthy scene made me *so hard* I was late for a meeting. Who would have thought?" He slides further in and stops just at the back of my throat, so I have to keep completely still to avoid activating my gag reflex. "But you got one thing wrong," he continues. "That's when I realized you'd never tried any of the things you wrote. It was all just a fantasy. Because there's no way to breathe with a dildo deep in your throat. Not even through your nose."

He tuts and pulls his finger back as slowly as it entered. "That was when I knew I had to teach you." He gives a tap under my chin to close my mouth, and when he releases my throat, the trance breaks.

I swallow hard. "It's just a fantasy. I don't want any of that in real life."

"Are you sure about that?"

"Yes. It's like rape fantasies. Most women have them. That doesn't mean they want to be raped." I squeeze my eyes shut and hold my breath as I realize what I'm saying. The r-word. He's going to do that to me. And now I just put the idea right at the front of his mind.

I startle as his knuckles brush my cheek. "I'm not going to rape you," he says in the softest voice as he repeats the motion.

"Then... What—" The words stick in my throat as I choke up. I'm not sure if it's the fear of not knowing what he has planned, the softness of his touch, or his promise not to violate me, but tears brim around the contact lenses as the shock, fear, shame, and vulnerability crash together inside me. All those emotions have been there all along since I woke up in this dark nightmare. They have been simmering underneath the surface, but the drug he gave me had numbed me to the impact, and now it slams into me with delayed effect. Suddenly, the tears are slipping down my cheeks and I'm sniffling and whimpering. I feel utterly wretched, but there's nowhere to hide. When I turn my face, he pushes it back with a gentle nudge on my chin.

I try to lift an arm over my face instead, but he takes my wrists and moves my arms to my sides. He doesn't use force, but I'm sure he'll tighten his grip the moment I try to rip them free, so I remain still as defeat becomes a heavy weight on my chest. I grow all too aware of how much he sees. I can't see anything, but he can see everything. My quivering lips, my shaky chest, and the tears that keep streaming out of my eyes. All my fear and vulnerability is painted in vivid colors.

"I'm not going to rape you," he repeats as he

leans close and presses his lips to my wet cheek. He does the same to the other side, kissing the wet streak of tears. "I know that part of the story is not supposed to come true." He says it with so much understanding and genuineness that I want to believe him.

But how can I? How can I believe anything he says when he has drugged me, kidnapped me, and made me into this helpless creature?

What he says next is supposed to be a reassurance—words to prove his sincerity—but it has the exact opposite effect. He releases my arms to cup my face between his hands, and his hot breath heats my lips as he hovers right in front of me. "By the time I shove my dick inside you, you'll be begging for it."

He touches my lips with a soft kiss the moment I cry out.

"No!" The agonized wail thrusts me into a turbulent stream of desperation. I sob as I writhe on the mattress, shoving my hands against his chest as I kick the comforter off and jerking my neck against the chain. Then I roam my hands all over—my throat, the chain, the sheets. I'm not sure what I'm searching for, and I don't find anything. All I feel is restrictive leather, keeping my hands trapped in perpetual fists. I blink my eyes wildly, needing to see. It doesn't matter what. My desperation has no purpose anymore. I just need to get out of this black helplessness—get my sight back and move my hands.

My sobs grow ever more desperate as claustrophobia closes in. My breathing moves in shallow gusts of air, and a haze infiltrates my brain to eradicate all logical thought and instill blinding panic.

"No!" I scream as a hand splays over my chest.

"Breathe," a voice says, but the blaring alarm bells in my mind drown out the sound.

I shove at the arm and cry harder as I'm once again confronted with the humiliating state of my hands.

A weight presses down on my chest, and I can't get air into my lungs. I vaguely register that it's not the hand compressing my chest that blocks my air, but it doesn't matter. I can't breathe, and I writhe and flail as I heave for air without catching any.

"Breathe," the same voice repeats with more force, but the alarms in my head have grown in volume too.

Suddenly, I'm off the mattress, in a lap. Strong arms close tightly around me. "Breathe," a voice urges right next to my ear. It's deep and steady, and it carries through the blaring alarm bells with a willful resonance.

I drag in a breath so hard my entire body shudders with the effort.

"One more," the voice says as arms tighten around me.

Against all logic, the tight sensation doesn't hinder my breath. Rather, it pulls me into my body and makes me feel the swoosh of air rushing through my chest as I inhale deeply. My sobbing stops as I turn my focus to my airways and the tight sensation that steadies me through the storm. I heave ragged breaths and notice how the arms slacken slightly, then tighten again as I push the air out through quivering lips.

"Good girl," he whispers against my ear and kisses my cheek. "Keep going. Just like that."

I do as he says. I don't think about who's holding me or why I couldn't breathe in the first place. My world is reduced to the simple act of breathing. In and out. In and out.

Somewhere along the way, I begin to notice little things—like the thumb stroking my arm in soothing caresses, the scent of cologne and scotch that drifts into my senses with each spoken "Good girl," and the press of tiny buttons of a dress shirt at my back.

Gradually, I grow cognizant of the bigger things—the strong arms that band around me, his body pressing against mine, and his heat that seems to radiate straight into my shuddery body. It's tight and confining, yet it chases away my claustrophobia and wraps me in a cocoon of safety.

I stay there for a while, just breathing, as I drop my head back onto a shoulder and close my eyes. Everything is calm. Until my brain recovers and thoughts filter back in.

I stir slightly to get free, and he lets me crawl out of his arms to sit on my own.

The strange affection must have made me hopeful because my words don't feel pointless when I say, "Will you please let me go?"

He presses his hands to my back in a soothing gesture. "No."

I lift my arms and burrow my head into my elbows as my breath shudders past my lips, threatening to bring more tears.

"Come here." Pulling gently at my arms, he urges me back against his body.

I don't protest. I'm too exhausted and need to save whatever little strength I have left, so I sink back into him and let him run his hands up and down my arms. The motion is alluring. There's so much affection in his touch that I can almost forget what this is. At first, he's only rubbing my arms, but as I sink into him, he starts moving his hands around, stroking my cheeks, stroking my neck, and smoothing the hair from my face. It's caring and protective in a way that reminds me of a lover's touch, and as he keeps going, patiently chasing away the shivers, it gets harder to remember that he's my captor and kidnapper—not my lover.

"How did you find the story?" I ask at some point, needing to break the spell so I won't forget what this is.

"How did I find it?" he parrots. "You mean,

how did I discover you were keeping filthy secrets, or how did I access them?"

"I don't know. Both."

He hums like he's about to tell me a fond memory. "I didn't even have to read the story to figure you out. When you're at your computer at lunch, biting your lip, and your cheeks turn as red as your favorite dress"—he presses a hand to my cheek, which must be said color too now—"and warm as the vanilla chai tea you drink. It's written all over your pretty face, really."

"You're someone from work," I conclude as my muddled brain processes his words.

He taps my nose. "You're as smart as you're pretty." With a bemused chuckle, he adds, "Well, in some ways. Leaving your dirty fantasies on your work computer wasn't very smart, now, was it?"

My head works overtime as I go through my colleagues, one by one, while trying to listen for more clues in his words. *Think, think, think.* Who would want to take me? I can't think of anyone who might hold a grudge. Rosa might get competitive at times and jealous that I'm headed for a promotion and she isn't, but I can't think of any men who might want some kind of strange revenge. But this doesn't seem to be about revenge; rather crazed attraction.

"Are you Brent?" I blurt, feeling stupid even as the words come out, and even stupider when he lets out a hearty laugh.

"Brent? Are you serious? That man couldn't pull something like this off even if he wanted to. You'd be in that dingy basement you wrote about now. Or more likely, he'd be in jail, and you'd be home in your own bed, slightly shaken, but no worse for wear."

"Then who arc you?"

He strokes my cheek affectionately as he says without humor, "Someone who wants to fulfill all your dirty desires."

CHAPTER 4

He places me flat on my stomach, then proceeds to pour something thick and oily over my skin, which I realize must be massage oil as he goes to work on my stiff muscles.

I try to remain tense and refuse his ministrations, but his capable hands roam all over my body—my back, my arms, my legs, and even my feet—with just the right pressure, and I'm too exhausted to keep up the resistance. Before long, I give in to the sensations and let him drag me into a floaty space.

When he stops, I'm loose in every joint and muscle—so relaxed I could sleep despite everything. I'm about to drift off when he pulls the comforter over my back and sits at the foot of the bed, sliding his hand under the comforter to stroke my thighs. I barely even realize he has nudged my thighs apart until a finger touches my folds.

"Hmm, you like being touched." He slides the finger in between my folds, and I stiffen as he holds it there. "Or maybe you're still wet from when I grabbed your neck."

"I don't want any of this," I protest.

"No?" The mattress dips as he crawls over me, and I feel his face hover close to mine. "Open your mouth."

"Why?"

He lowers his voice to a dangerous tone. "Open. Your. Mouth."

I part my lips, just a smidgen. I don't dare open up and find out what he's going to do, but I don't dare disobey either.

He slides his finger inside, nudging my teeth apart as he goes. The moment he presses the slick digit onto my tongue, I jerk my head back, but he anticipates my reaction and blocks my retreat with his other hand. Fisting my hair, he holds my head in place as he drags his finger back and forth over my tongue, turning it around to make sure I lap up every last drop of my own juices.

I whimper and pound my trapped hands into the mattress as the musky taste spreads over my tongue. I jerk my head, but he only grips my hair tighter, making my scalp burn and my neck strain backward in an awkward position.

"Tell me you're not just a little turned on," he rasps against my ear.

I try to shake my head, but it's impossible, so I just groan around his finger.

He pulls out and slips his finger back between

my folds, sliding it back and forth without touching my opening directly. He adds another digit, and this time, he moves straight toward my opening, slowly and purposefully. Panic grips me just as he's about to push inside.

"You said you wouldn't rape me!" I yell.

He pauses and leans close to my ear again. "What is your definition of rape?"

"Sexual abuse." I try to squirm farther up on the mattress to free myself from the imminent intrusion, but he pins me in place with a knee on my back.

"Yes, but is it any sort of penetration, or does it have to be cock in pussy? And is it abuse if the victim likes it?"

"I don't like it," I croak, frantic fear forcing my voice into a high pitch. "And it doesn't matter either way; I haven't consented."

He tuts. "Still not able to own up to your desires. I'll have to remedy that. But back to the matter at hand. Does the definition require intercourse, or will any kind of penetration make it rape?"

"Any kind," I whimper.

A sigh billows from his lips. "Sorry sweetheart, then I'm most definitely going to rape you." With a primal grunt, he slams his fingers inside and settles deep within me.

I scream into the room as desperation and degradation rip through my system. I try to squirm away, but I can't move. His fist in my hair has me straining backward, trapped in a tense position. All I can do is hang there, panting as the echo of my scream hovers in the air and the violation throbs through my body. My chest shakes as I try to process the shock, but it's too much, too sudden. My mind still hasn't recovered from the drugs and refuses to cope with the violation, so it shuts down and goes as black as my vision.

Gently, he lowers my head to the mattress and smooths my tangled hair from my face. He switches between stroking my cheek with the back of his hand and grazing the sensitive spot behind my ear with his fingertips. Silence settles over the room as he holds me there, impaled on his fingers, caressing me with deceptive tenderness. Blackened as my mind is, I'm barely cognizant of the discrepancy, and soon my body starts reacting to his touch. The shudders in my chest fade, and tingling sensations skitter down my neck as the rest of my body relaxes.

"Good girl," he whispers. "So pretty. So helpless." He presses a soft kiss to my temple. "I like that very much."

Something stirs inside me. I'm not sure where it comes from or how it got there, but a spark flickers at his appraisal. I want that. To be desired and to please.

He leans down to kiss my neck, alternating between bites and nibbles, licks and brushes of his lips. "I love how you surrender even though you don't want to. And I love the way your body awakens beneath my touch. Just like I imagined it would."

My breathing deepens as heat thaws the frozen defeat in my chest. The warmth radiates through my body to stir up a tingling sensation deep in my belly and to soothe the nervous chill in my skin. When he moves his fingers inside me, I realize I had all but forgotten about them. Something stirs at the back of my mind, wanting me to remember the violation, but my world is shrouded in a darkness that makes it easy to pretend it's just a dream—a strange dream that takes me from nightmarish realms to sweet lands in the blink of an eye as dreams often do.

He moves his fingers in and out at a languid pace as he continues the kissing and stroking. Sensations seep into my body from both ends to crash together at my core, where they stir up an electric buzzing.

I moan, craning my neck to give him better access. I want more. More of the sweet touches, more of the languid strokes, and maybe even more than that—something I can't give voice to.

"Such a good girl," he croons as he slowly slides his hand onto my throat like he did before. As he goes, he repositions himself to lie behind me, pulling me into a little spoon as he licks the edges of my ear. "Will you do as I say from now on?"

"Yes," I moan.

He lets out a low chuckle. "I don't believe you, but that's okay. I'll make sure you obey one way or another."

"Hmm," is all I can get out, and I'm not even sure I know what I'm responding to. It's all so hazy. All I know is the sensations in my body—the hand pressing against my windpipe, the delicious strokes of the fingers along my inner walls, and the tingly sensations at my ear.

"Would you like to come?" he asks.

"Yes." My breathing grows heavier, and my hips grind as he presses his palm against my clit. The electric sensations coil in my belly, building like a brewing storm, yet the rest of my body is free and open in a way it never has been when I was about to come. My moans grow louder as I feel myself hover at the precipice.

"Yesss," I say on a long exhale coming from deep within my stomach.

But then it all stops. The fingers withdraw, the hand releases my neck, and his strong body disappears.

It's like falling and crashing onto concrete ground. Confusion and unfulfilled desire twist in my body, and suddenly, I'm shaking again. I try to sit up, but my neck catches on the chain, and I fall back. I don't know what's going on. It's like I'm waking up from a nightmare. A dream full of eerie black visions with shimmers of light and shadows.

Strange voices and contradictory emotions.

I try to open my eyes, but everything remains black. I turn my head, and there's that same vision as in the dream: the globe of light at the side, an outline of something like an armchair, and a shadow moving before me.

"Please," I say, reaching for it, not knowing what I'm begging for. Maybe something to ground me. A little comfort to fend off the despair that shudders to get out. "Please," I repeat, feeling the pounding need between my legs. "I—I need to come."

A hand settles on my lower arm, and I try to curl my fingers around the man's wrist, needing to hold on to something. But my fist won't open, and suddenly, it all slams back into me with terrifying clarity: Darkness might pervade both my sight and mind, but I'm wide awake—at the mercy of this stranger.

I try to pull my arm away, but he tightens his grip. "I'm sorry," he says with genuine regret, "but you haven't earned an orgasm yet."

"Please," I cry into the room as tears fill my eyes. "I can't take this anymore."

"Shh, I'll take care of you." He pulls the comforter over me.

"No, you won't," I say with incredulous despair. "You're crushing me."

"I'm not," he says like he truly believes it. "I'm freeing you. You might not be able to see that now, but you'll get there."

"No, I won't." My voice grows louder, more desperate. "There's nothing freeing about any of this. It's crushing, fucked-up, and cruel."

"Shh-sh-shh," is his only response, and I go silent and draw in on myself because it's all so very hopeless.

CHAPTER 5

He leaves me alone in the room for a while, maybe to let me process or because he needs to do something—prepare whatever comes next. I don't know. When he returns, he fumbles with the chain on the collar, and there's a click, like a padlock popping open. "Come. Up, off the bed." He slides a hand under my back to help me up.

I gingerly scoot to the edge of the bed, place my feet on the floor, and lean into his supportive grip on my arm as I get up. Grabbing both my arms from behind, he slowly leads me forward. My legs carry me with tiny steps. They're weak and I'm blind, not sure I trust this man to make sure I won't bump into something.

He stops me after a short while. "I want you to kneel for me. I'm not going to do anything; I just want you to sit there for a while and feel the power difference."

I give a confused shake of my head. It sounds like a hoax. Why would he want me to simply kneel?

He helps me to the floor, and I willingly bend my legs to fall into position. He could ask so much worse of me, so I'm not going to waste my strength fighting him on this.

My confusion only grows when my knees land on something soft. A sheepskin, I think.

"Now, straighten your back and lower your chin." With a hand against my spine and one against my chest, he adjusts my posture, then presses a finger to the indentation above my chin to lower my head. "Hands on your thighs."

I obey as I sense him step in front of me, and then I just sit there. Nothing happens. No words, no movement. Just me kneeling before him like he said.

At first, I'm tense, expecting some kind of sudden change—humiliation, maybe pain. I don't know what this man wants or is capable of. But when he places a hand on top of my head, things begin to change. My trust in this strange peace builds, and I allow myself to relax.

"Shoulders back," he corrects when I slouch. Besides that, there are no words.

I become increasingly aware of my position—the humbleness of kneeling in front of him with my head bowed. I can't see him, but I can clearly sense him, towering above me, powerful and willful.

Like a deity and his disciple.

The thought sends a twisty sensation to my stomach. It's wrong. I shift as this strange act takes on new meaning, badly wanting to pull away completely.

"Sit still." He strokes his hand across my hair a few times.

I tense my shoulders instead, but he orders me to relax them and does the same when I tighten my jaw.

"Deep breaths," he orders and guides my breathing, in through the nose and out through the mouth.

I obey each time, still of the mind to save my struggling for something that will actually hurt me.

But even though this isn't harmful, it's by no means inconsequential, I slowly realize. Something happens as I sit there with my muscles loose and my breaths deep. The stillness pulls me into my body, awakening a floaty sensation—light, yet heavy and grounded. I once again notice the humbleness of my lowered head and kneeling position, and a gust of emotion billows through me.

I can't put my finger on what it is, but it's something deep and important. A desire that reaches beyond something sexual. It's something that tugs at that same place where the urge to please sparked.

"Can you feel the humility?" he asks like he

senses the change in me.

I bite my lips, not wanting to admit it, but I can't make myself lie either, so I end up giving a nod.

He lets out a pleased hum and slides his hand to the back of my head, pulling it forward so my forehead rests against his thigh.

I want to dart up and flee, because the feeling that swooshes through me scares me. Before I can do it, he locks his hand onto my nape above the collar, firm yet gentle. I don't have it in me to resist, but it's no longer because I want to save my strength. It's because he has me spellbound—entranced in this potent moment of power and humility. Master and servant. God and disciple.

"Can you feel that your will doesn't matter anymore?" He tightens his grip on my nape. "You're mine, and all that matters is my command."

A tear slips from my eyes. Because this is wrong. It's all so very fucking wrong. Yet I can't deny the strength of this odd pull between us: I can't deny his words.

I don't respond, and I don't think he needs me to because he already knows the answer.

CHAPTER 6

When he helps me back onto the bed, I'm pliant in body and mind. I move however he wants and obediently lean my head back to let him reattach the chain.

"Good girl. You deserve a reward for that pretty submission."

Is that what this was? Submission? I want to ask him, but I can't seem to form the words.

He attaches the leather mittens to the collar with a short chain that traps my hands at the top of my chest—traps me even deeper under his command. This time, the helplessness isn't as devastating as I felt it earlier. It's just there. Or maybe even more so, it pulls me further into that floaty sensation I'm still hovering in.

He crawls between my legs, and I let him push them apart. A gust of hot breath tickles my folds just before his wet tongue slides over them.

A gasp escapes me as my nether region sparks alive. It's like a flick of a switch. A moment ago, I didn't even notice a tingling sensation down there, but now the entire area is pulsing and pounding. He finds my swollen nub with his tongue, and I cry out as lust flares in my sensitive nerve endings.

"Oh God, oh God," I moan as he keeps licking. My hands shake against my chest, but it's not from exhaustion or fear this time. It's from overpowering, overwhelming desire. I badly crave more—a finger inside me, maybe two. I want to beg him as he keeps licking, but I can't let go of the memory of how I got here—the wrongness of it all—so I just lie there, moaning and writhing as the need grows to explosive heights.

I've never been able to come from the simple touch of a tongue, but as he keeps going, swirling around my clit and licking along my sensitive folds, I draw closer to the edge. My toes curl as pleasure shoots in shuddery jolts through my body.

"Yes, please, more," I say as a tightening sensation is about to set the orgasm rolling.

But then he stops.

I try to close my legs and grind them together—I just need a little more friction—but he holds them apart.

"No, no, no, no, no. Please don't—please don't stop." I burst into a frantic tirade of begging and whimpering. My mind feels like it's about to combust under the pressure as my body pulses with the need for release. But no relief is to be found.

"Not yet," is all he says, and I want to cry. I try not to—I really do—but I just can't help it. The denial is too harsh. Tears trail from my eyes, and I turn my head from side to side, whimpering with the need to hide, but I can't even do that. Once the convulsing in my body stops, no longer threatening to send me over at the slightest touch, he crawls over me and grabs my jaw.

"You're so beautiful when you cry," he says, almost reverently. I can all but feel his eyes boring into me, taking in every little nuance of my vulnerability and desperation.

"This is sick. You're si—" My words break off because I can't find any conviction to put behind them. I let out a broken sound as I realize it's not him. "I'm the one who's sick," I mutter so quietly I don't think he hears.

He leans in to speak directly into my ear. "You're not sick. You're the most beautiful creature I've ever seen."

"No, it's wrong. I shouldn't like any of this."

"Says who?"

"I—everyone. I don't know."

"It doesn't matter what everyone else thinks. No one can see you. It's only me, and I find your submission beautiful and moving. It's a gift."

Shaking my head, I part my lips to say something, but no words come out. What he's saying makes no sense, and I don't know how to respond.

"I wasn't sure if I could make you submit like that." He leans his forehead against mine. "Like when you knelt before me. I saw the potential in your stories—even in your disposition—but not everyone has the strength to let go like that even though the desire is there. But you did."

I barely understand the full meaning of his words, but I grasp the magnitude. Amidst all the wrongness, the violation, and humiliation, I feel special and cherished. It doesn't make sense, and somehow it doesn't have to. I relax beneath him and breathe a sigh of surrender. A few more tears drip from my eyes, but it's as much from the powerful surge of submission as from anything else. It's a strange and new sensation, and I'm not sure if I'm okay with it, but it doesn't matter at this moment.

"There it is again," he says, completely in tune with my reactions even though he doesn't know me. And that's the exact same way I feel with him as he presses his mouth to my lips: It's a perfect connection—the missing piece I never knew I needed. Like yin and yang, creating balance in imbalance. Black and white. Good and bad.

He pushes past my lips and starts a languid dance of our tongues. His lips are soft, his clean-shaven skin the same, and he tastes as exquisite as a fifty-year-old scotch. Woodsy with a hint of caramel. And God, he can kiss. It's soft yet dominating, leaving no doubt as to who's in charge even as he makes me feel beautiful and desired. His hands curve around my cheeks with affectionate tenderness as he sucks gently on my lips and licks at my tongue. Then he slides his hands into my hair and plunges his tongue deep into my mouth, moving against mine in a way that makes it impossible to reciprocate. All I can do is open up and let him take.

"I'm not through with you," he groans against my lips. "I've yet to show you how complete my power becomes when I shove a dildo down your throat."

I moan into his mouth as he robs me of breath with another deep kiss.

With a groan, he pulls away, like he's struggling to control himself, and his voice is deep and raspy when he speaks again. "I'm gonna fill all of your holes, and then you're gonna beg for my cock."

The bed bounces as he jumps off and leaves the room, giving me no time to answer.

I lie panting as I wait, reeling from the intensity of... everything. The submission, the kiss, his promise. I can barely form a coherent thought, and all resistance seems to have vanished into a black hole, leaving only this strange new sensation that is submission.

Anticipation and fear coalesce inside me as the door opens and he approaches the bed.

"Spread your legs," he growls, spurring me

into obedience.

He jumps up over me, unlocks the mittens from the collar, and slams my wrists into the mattress. The rough edge in his voice becomes a full growl as he leans into my face. "Can you feel how helpless you are? I've taken your sight, your touch, and even your ability to think." He gathers both my wrists in one hand above my head and presses a finger to my forehead. "I've inserted myself right here, and there's no way you'll ever get me out."

I believe him. The realization is as terrifying as it is electrifying. Because I have no idea what will happen after this night. He said he would set me free. Does that mean I won't see him again—or that I'll see him at work without ever knowing it's him?

The thought sends a dreadful burst of fear through my system, but as he flips me over and spits between my ass cheeks, whatever fear was in my mind a moment ago is replaced by a new one.

"What are you doing?" I cry out.

"Like I told you, I'm filling all of your holes." He presses a finger into the spit and uses the moisture as lubricant as he circles my narrow opening. "I'm making you mine, through and through."

I gasp as a whole new bunch of nerves flare alive. I never knew so much sensation could exist back there. It goes straight through my pelvis, awakening the entire area, but I'm terrified of getting something into *that* opening. “I don’t think I can take it.”

“Yes, you can.” He presses the tip of his finger inside without warning.

“No,” I beg, squirming to break the connection.

He smacks his other hand down on my ass. “Keep still.” All gentleness that seems to have accompanied everything he’s done until this point—even the cruel things—is suddenly gone. Left is only primal hunger. It scares me to the core, yet it feeds the raging need inside me. But when he pushes in to the second knuckle, I can’t repress the rising panic. My mind and body just won’t cooperate. The gnawing fear overrides the pulsing need. I start to squirm, shoving my hands back to push at him as I beg him to stop.

He pulls out and jumps off the bed, and I don’t know whether to be disappointed or relieved. *Lost,* is what I feel the most. But the feeling doesn’t last long. As he grabs one of my hands, the connection blazes alive anew. He’s rough as he fastens my wrists to the headboard, but I don’t care. All that matters is his control. It seeps into me and grounds me in a way nothing ever has even as it throws my world into chaos. I want it; I don’t want it.

I need it.

Plastic crackles. Latex, I realize as he grabs my ass cheek with a gloved hand and drips cold lube onto my opening.

“Oh God. *Fuck.* No, no, no.” I can’t stop my

pleading string of words as he smears the lube around my opening and presses the tip of a gloved finger inside.

"Has anyone ever been in here before?" He pushes a little deeper.

"No," I gasp.

"Good," he growls. He massages a little before pressing deeper, and I whimper as the invasion becomes all I feel. He's not just invading that forbidden hole. It's everything: my mind, my body, my very sense of self. I can't contain anything as new sensations burst alive around the intrusion. When he's knuckle-deep, I feel shattered—broken apart and torn open. I start shaking all over. My very foundation has shifted, and I can't figure anything out. But I don't have to.

With a warm hand on my back, he grants me the stability I desperately need. "I've got you," he says, once again reading my reactions perfectly.

"I don't think I can take any more."

"Yes, you can," he says with such certainty I almost believe him.

He pulls out his finger and applies more lubricant before pressing two digits against my narrow opening. I'm about to burst into another stream of pleas, but he predicts it and shoves the urge right back.

"This hole is mine now," he says with a force that renders me speechless. He presses back in, straight past my sphincter, and I squeeze my eyes shut as a burning sensation flares in my tight muscle. "I'll do whatever I want to it, and you'll take it. Are we clear?"

"Yes," I groan, half moan.

He only spends a minute this time, working himself all the way in. Pain swirls into a flood of pleasure, mixing like they're perfect companions. He drags his fingers in and out a few times, and the sensation is so sharp my moans turn into loud cries that fill the room with desperation and need.

It only gets worse when he replaces his fingers with a cold metal butt plug. Sweat beads on my brow as he begins the slow process of working it into my ass. Unable to take the burst of sensations and pain, I writhe and arch above the mattress, shaking and jerking as I beg him to stop.

He moves onto my back, holding me in place with his weight as he reaches down to continue the unmerciful advance, stretching my narrow walls with the plug. Not even having my legs free and kicking makes a difference. He continues just the same, and there's nothing I can do about it.

"It doesn't fit," I scream one moment, then beg him quietly as tears sting my eyes. "Please stop, I can't take it."

He doesn't speak until the plug pops in place, seated deep inside me as a constant, throbbing reminder of who now owns that hole. All energy seems to fade from me in one fell swoop as defeat knocks into me. I go slack on the bed. But the defeat is not crushing this time. Rather, it's freeing, letting me live in the thoughtless world of powerlessness, accepting that I'm no longer the master of my own body.

I'm limp and pliant when he turns me on the bed to lie on my back, my hands still trapped to the headboard. When he presses a finger against my bottom lip, I willingly open up, and I keep going as he presses, coaxing my mouth wide open. My breathing speeds up as he shoves something between my teeth and locks it in place with straps that he buckles at the back of my head. It's not a regular gag ball, though, or even a muzzle. Inspecting the thing with my tongue, I find that it's more like a short, wide tube. An opening.

Realization strikes when he prods a dildo between my slick folds. He must read the reaction on my face because he says, "You know what's going to happen, don't you?"

A garbled sound escapes me as I try to reply.

It doesn't take many moments of prodding to get the toy inside. It easily slides through my juices, filling me to the brim as it moves against the plug on the other side of my thin inner wall. I pant hard as he drags it in and out a few times, whipping my head from side to side as I try to process the overwhelming sensations that keep building to the point where I can't control anything. Not my moans, my screams, or the violent jerks in my body—nor the drool that spills down my cheeks.

He finally pulls the dildo out and steps around the bed, close to my face. I see him as a tall shadow in the globe of light as he leans over me and tuts. "Such a dirty girl, drooling all over my sheets. I'd better block that filthy hole of yours before you make an even bigger mess."

With a hand on my forehead, he holds me in place, and I'm all too aware of what he's doing. I sense the dildo even before it reaches my tongue. The air passing into my mouth thins out, the tube moves as he inserts the dildo, and a musky scent fills my nose. I whimper and jerk my head against his hand, but the dildo sinks into my mouth just the same. The tip connects with my tongue, and my whimpers grow more desperate as I try to fold it back to avoid the taste of myself. But there's no avoiding, only postponing. Tightening his hand around my jerking head, he presses the toy farther in, and soon the full length slides over my tongue.

I writhe on the mattress, squirming and accidentally squeezing my muscles around the intrusion in my ass. I cry out, but the sound dies as he presses the dildo against the back of my throat. From then on, it's only garbled sounds that escape me and drool spilling from the corners of my mouth.

Panic grabs at me as my gag reflex stutters, and I jerk at the chains holding my wrists.

"Relax your throat," he demands. A smirk

sounds in his voice as he adds, "Or you'll have more than drool down your chin in a minute."

I freeze every muscle except for the ones in my throat as I try to relax around the intrusion. It helps, but it takes all my focus, and I feel helpless to the bone as I give up the fight and let the dildo advance into my throat. Tears stream from my eyes as he fills my throat and snuffs out my breath. I heave for air, but everything is blocked. Shock and horror must be written all over my face.

"See?" he mocks. "No air at all."

I barely hear his words as I rage an inner battle against my gag reflex, trying to remain calm even as panic tugs at every muscle inside me, wanting me to thrash and writhe. I want to beg him with my eyes, but everything remains black. Empty. I'm all alone in this void. No air, no light, no movement. Nothing.

"Focus on my touch." He smooths his hand over my forehead and keeps going in soothing motions, and it pulls me back to him, out of the claustrophobic loneliness.

"You have enough air to go a moment longer. Just relax."

I take stock of my lungs and realize he's right. I'm not desperate for air yet, so I give in. I let go and let him take control of my most basic need and yet another intimate opening. The acceptance pulls me back into that strange, floaty place, and when he pulls out and starts the process all over, I find myself sinking into his steady control, willingly relaxing to let the dildo in.

"Good girl. So pretty. So submissive." He keeps stroking my hair as he goes two more times. Then he shoves the toy back into my pussy and drives me toward the peak with painfully slow drags along my inner walls. *In, out. In, out.* I spasm violently and cry out as my muscles contract around the intrusions that fill me to the brim.

"Are you ready to ask for my cock?"

I nod my head eagerly as I unproblematically hurl the plea for him to fuck me out. But the words are garbled and nonsensical as I sputter around the gag.

"I need to hear it." He loosens the gag and takes it out just long enough for me to say the words.

"Please, fuck me." I try to close my mouth and swallow the drool, but he sticks his fingers into my mouth and shoves the gag straight back in.

"Filthy girl." He smears the saliva across my cheek. "Maybe I should just come on your face since you're already such a mess." He drags the drool at the other side of my mouth up over my other cheek too. "But I promised to take you when you asked for it."

Jumping up on the bed, he climbs between my legs. The sound of a zipper rips through the silence, followed by the rustle of fabric and the sound of rubber as I think he sheathes his cock.

But what dips inside me is not his cock. It's the dildo.

I groan in disappointment.

"I promised to fill all three holes too." He slips the toy all the way in before dragging it out. Then the musky scent of my lust fills my senses as he shoves the dildo back into my mouth. Wasting no time, he presses his erection against my opening, and I cry out around the gag as hot need bursts through me. I'm not aware of how badly I need him until he pushes inside, filling me to the brim with his thick erection. It's like a shot of adrenaline through my system. I imagine this is what it must be like for an addict to go without their favorite drug for days, then getting a shot straight into a vein.

He draws back out with a groan more animal than man. Then he shoves back inside, slowly, while pushing the toy in my mouth deeper at the same pace. Frantic energy bursts through my system as bolts of sensation shoot through me from all ends. The plug rubs against my narrow walls as his cock slides inside, filling me to the point where I'm about to burst, and the dildo does the same to my mouth, filling me to the brim, snuffing out my breath, and invading my senses with the taste of my own desire. All along, my emotions rage through me, needing this stranger's power over me the same way I need air.

I go still as he sinks to the hilt and settles the

dildo deep within my throat. A breathless moment passes before he starts moving inside me. Desire explodes through me, driving me close to the peak in a matter of seconds.

But then he stops. Just like he did the other times I was about to come. Desperation builds inside me, but I can't get it out since I have to remain still to avoid choking on the cruel invasion in my throat. He just stays there, deeply rooted inside me, physically and mentally. My air runs dry, little by little, and panic creeps along the edges of my mind. I bang my trapped fists into the mattress above my head, shaking all over.

He pulls back his cock until the tip hovers right inside my opening. Then suddenly, he yanks the dildo out just as he shoves himself back into my pussy. Air swooshes into my lungs like a blaze of fire as my nether region explodes in a torrent of sensation. I scream into the room, over and over, as the orgasm tears through my body.

His growls blend with my screams, and his cock grows impossibly thick as he slows to jerky movements inside me.

Then my world sinks into heavy, peaceful silence as he pulls out and I collapse on the mattress, limp in every bone and muscle.

CHAPTER 7

"Are you okay?"

I stir from the calm darkness at the sound of a deep voice. Blinking my eyes, I find I'm still blind, but it's not as scary this time as I lean into the protective hand stroking my cheek.

"I'm okay." My jaw aches as I speak, and I realize the gag is gone. So is the butt plug, I register as I clench my inner muscles and wince at the raw feeling that awakens down there. The mittens remain on my hands, though.

"Is it okay if I hold you?"

"Uhm, sure. Why are you asking?"

"Easy as you were to read during play, it's always harder to read someone who's in subspace, and your stories all end before aftercare."

I feel him make himself comfortable on the mattress beside me, then he pulls me to his chest—facing him this time—and flips the comforter over us. Pressing a finger under my chin, he tips my head up to kiss my lips. “I also don’t want to end this night on a bad note.”

“What happens when the night is over?”

He tucks my head back into his chest and holds me close like I’m precious to him. “I’ll take you home.”

Tons of questions swirl in my mind. *And then what? Will I ever see you again?* But all the most pressing ones make me too emotional—I’m not ready to admit that I badly want to see him again—so I settle for asking the most puzzling one. “Aren’t you afraid I’ll go to the police?”

“Not really.” Pressing his cheek against the top of my head, he wraps a leg over mine. “I’m still gonna take my precautions, though. But right now, I need to make sure you’re okay. We still have a little time before the sun comes up.”

“Why sunrise?”

He seems to consider for a moment. “It seems poetic.”

His embrace is soothing and safe despite everything, and I don’t want to ruin the moment by asking more questions, so I hold them in.

I almost drift off as I lie there, nestled against his body. He’s still fully clothed, but his heat radiates through the barrier of fabric to warm my naked skin, and his arms feel strong around me, his chest wide and solid. I imagine someone who works out regularly and takes good care of himself.

A beautiful, masculine man. He's tall too—easily wrapping me up in a cocoon. If I had felt his size and rippling muscles at the beginning of the night, it would have instilled more terror within me, but as I lie here, it's like a shield of protection.

I have no idea how I got here. *This man raped me.* He forced himself upon me when I screamed for him to stop, yet I badly want to feel him now. A little voice in my head tells me I'm sick, but when I recall the way he shoved the shame back when I said those words out loud, the voice fades away. It doesn't matter what I *should* feel; all that matters is that I've somehow come to trust this man on some warped level. I'm not sure if it was the kneeling, his strange gentleness, or maybe the way he played my body like an instrument he'd mastered to perfection, but somewhere along the way, he turned my body as well as my mind against me and made them his.

His.

He told me I'm his.

A small smile plays on my lips, and I snuggle a bit closer to him, relishing the feeling of his arms tightening around me as he hums with contentment. *He actually hums.* Who would have thought a man like this likes to cuddle? I can hardly believe it, but there's no doubting it as he strokes his hand along my back and presses a tender kiss to the top of my head.

"Ten more minutes, and then we need to get

you cleaned up." He tightens his grip like he doesn't want to let go, and I give a discontented grunt because I don't want to leave this warm closeness either.

Ten minutes pass way too quickly. Before long, he's off the bed, unlocking the collar, and helping me to my feet. I feel more naked than I have all night as he removes the metal band from my neck. It's a terrible symbol of where I'm headed—away from his control. I swallow a knot in my throat and reach for him.

He takes my hand, granting me the connection I badly need, and wraps an arm around my waist. But as he guides me out of the room, I feel the end closing in, and his touch is no longer enough to dispel the unease simmering in my gut. We walk through a long space that must be a hallway, and the blackness of my vision softens into gray shades as he leads me through a door to a brightly lit room. Cool tile under my feet reveals it's a bathroom.

"Sit." He guides me to a toilet, and I lower my head and hug my arms awkwardly around myself as I feel him towering above me. "Go ahead," he adds when I just sit there.

"Will you please leave while I... do my business?"

He huffs a laugh and presses a finger under my chin as he leans close, his hot breath brushing my skin. "I've been inside your asshole, heard you scream with despair, and seen you lose all control as you came on my dick, and now you're worried that I see you pee?"

I bite my lips together and try to turn my head, but he grabs my jaw, locking my head in place. "Uh, uh, now you get to face me as you relieve yourself. It's almost a shame about the contacts. I'd love to see the embarrassment in your eyes as the sound of pee trickles into the toilet."

I let out a small whimper. "I don't need to pee."

Using his other hand, he prods three fingers into my stomach, right where my bladder is. "No?"

Clenching my inner muscles, I try to subdue the sudden urge to empty my bladder.

"You have one minute, or I'll enjoy watching you piss yourself in the shower."

Fuck. With a shuddery sigh, I give in and relax my inner muscles, but embarrassment makes it hard to let go completely, and it takes a while before I feel like I'm getting there.

"Ten, nine, eight," he starts counting.

"No, I'm trying," I protest, but he keeps going.

"Seven, six, five, four."

Finally, my body cooperates, and I pee. I try to control it so it won't hit the bowl as loudly, but there's no way to control the sound or speed. Blood gathers in my face as it keeps going, loud and clear.

"Good girl." He swipes his thumb along my

jaw. "Now you're pissing in front of me too. Next time, I just might pump water into your rear hole and watch you as you empty it into the toilet."

Next time. Flushing out my bowel! My head whirs as I try to figure out which one to latch on to, but I forget about it as he keeps up the humiliation. Shoving a hand between my legs, he wipes my folds thoroughly with a piece of toilet paper, and I burrow my head into my hands as shame heats my face.

Next, he leads me into a shower stall and fastens the mittens to something above me—a hook maybe. I jerk my arms to test the fixation when he steps away. No leeway. All I can do is blindly turn this way and that, and even a small step to the side forces me up on my toes. A whimper escapes me as I realize the helplessness that once again has me in its clutches.

Anxiousness creeps up my spine as I crane my neck to listen for sounds—any indication as to what's next. I almost expect him to hose me down with cold water, but instead of the sound of running water, there's a dry crackling sound, like latex gloves. It's the same sound as when he invaded my ass.

"What are you doing?" I yelp in a thin voice, clenching my butt as I expect another intrusion. "I can't take any more."

I feel him close in, and I jump at the feeling of a latex-clad hand on my cheek. "No more," he says softly as he curves his hand tenderly around the side of my face, but the barrier of the glove dilutes any sense of comfort his touch could provide. "But I need to clean you in case I misjudged you, and you do go to the police," he explains.

My stomach sinks. *Does he really think I might do that?* I can't even imagine it. I know it would be the sensible thing to do, but the thought of displeasing, let alone betraying him like that—the idea of never feeling the steadiness of his dominance and the safety of his arms again—has my stomach in knots.

He washes my entire body, and the longing for his touch is painful as he grants me this detached version of intimacy with the gloved hand. It's impersonal and practical, and so are the movements of his hands. All comfort and care is gone as he rids my body of any evidence that it was ever his. *Is* his? I don't know if it was just something he said or something he only meant for a limited time. It doesn't feel like either. My entire system feels like he has branded himself deeply into me, and having all traces of him washed away is a contradiction that scrapes my skin like sandpaper.

I try to sink into my head and recall the feeling of his tender touch—the loving way he stroked my skin—but the memory slips further and further away as he shoves a finger inside my ass to clean me there, then finishes by screwing the shower head loose and sticking the hose inside my pussy. The spray shoots into my sensitive folds, hurting me even as it awakens a desire as unwelcome as the one that blossomed the first time he touched me. Silent tears spill from my eyes as I squirm on tiptoes, trying to escape the hose. As with everything else tonight, it's useless. He simply grabs my hip with one hand, forcing me in place as he jams the hose deeper. The desire fades as the pain takes precedence, and I tense up with the effort of holding back the desperate sob that wants to rip from my throat and send me into fitful tears.

I somehow manage to hold myself together until he turns off the water and withdraws the hose, but the distance keeps growing and so does the need to break down.

He proceeds to brush my teeth thoroughly and make me gargle mouthwash before he takes me down and removes the mittens. My body is heavy and sluggish as I stagger out of the shower with the tiny help of his hand on my elbow. I don't know how I manage to stay upright as he helps me into my clothes, because everything inside me crumbles. My clothes smell like detergent as if he's washed them, and it's yet another thing that has my throat tightening with the prospect of losing him.

My shoulders slouch and my lips quiver as he cuffs my hands behind my back and leads me through the house, now wearing leather gloves instead of latex gloves. Tons of questions linger at the tip of my tongue, but I'm too devastated to ask any of them. I'm not even sure I want to know whether I'll get to be with him again, or if this is it. Right now, I just want to get away from him. Anything is better than this cold distance that has become a solid wall between us.

"Will you touch me one more time?" I beg when he takes off the cuffs and helps me into the back of a car, still blind.

He presses his hand to my cheek, but the leather of his glove eradicates all the affection that seems to be hidden behind the barrier.

"Please, without the glove," I choke out, swallowing hard to suppress the sudden urge to cry.

"I'm sorry," he says, sounding genuinely regretful as he removes his hand. "I can't do that." He pauses for a second, and his voice becomes detached. "Put on your seat belt."

The car door slams shut, and I draw in on myself as I descend into dark loneliness. Another door slams and there's a quiet whir, like a window going up or down, but no cold air seeps into the car.

"Take out the contact lenses," he says, and this time, his voice is muffled as if there's a barrier between us.

I have never worn contacts, but I've seen

Marie remove hers in the women's restroom more than once. Pulling up one eyelid, I find the lens with my other hand and try to pinch it. It takes a couple of tries before I get a hold of it and can remove it.

Blinking toward my surroundings, I see smooth brown leather, the inside of a car, and a black partition that is up.

Loneliness squeezes my chest as I take off the other lens. Finally, I can see. It should be a relief unlike any other, but it's not. All I want to do as I stare at the partition is put the lenses back in and beg the man on the other side to take me back.

But I don't. My throat is too tight to get any words out, anyway.

The car starts moving, and I stare out the window. At first, I think we must be on an unlit street and my sight still quite hasn't cleared up, but as I see no movement whatsoever, I realize the windows back here are blacked out. I'm as trapped as I was in the bed.

Tears pool in my eyes, and I quickly swipe them away. Then I just stare at my hands for several minutes. My open hands—free to use however I like. Why do I hate that so much?

I can't make sense of anything, and when he stops the car in front of my building, tells me to get out, and drives off, I just stand there at the side of the road, staring into space as daylight breaks. When I finally move, I'm shaking from the cold.

Even as I get inside and crawl into bed, I keep shuddering, and whatever sleep I get is fitful at best.

CHAPTER 8

"Did you get home safe Friday night?" Marie asks as she plops onto her chair beside me on Monday morning.

"Sure," I say without lifting my gaze from the computer screen.

"Rosa was so drunk she could barely walk." Marie lets out a laugh and keeps talking as she logs on to her computer to check her email while sipping coffee. It's the usual Monday morning routine, chit-chatting about our weekends while going through our messages. The only difference today is that I don't say a word.

When Marie has shared all the details of her crazy weekend, she turns to me for the first time since she came in. "Are you okay?" I feel her eyes assessing me, and her voice carries a hint of worry. "You don't look so good."

"Sorry, I'm just a bit under the weather." I force a smile and send it her way.

"Is that why you suddenly had to leave? You

were coming down with something?"

I nod. "I've been sick all weekend." It's not even that big of a lie. I may not have had a fever or a runny nose, but I've spent all weekend in bed, frozen in place, unable to do more than take care of my most urgent needs.

After deflecting more questions about my weekend, I spend the rest of Monday in a haze, working on routine, and avoiding small talk. I do manage to pull myself together and put on a smile for one whole hour for my presentation in the afternoon. The haze proves to almost be a blessing since it drowns out all the nervousness that would usually make my hands clammy and my mind all muddled. Today though, I can barely muster the will to care, and I just go in there and lay out my work—once again going on routine. Marie was right, I'm always overly prepared. Despite not having even peeked at my presentation during the weekend, I know just what to say. For a moment after I've finished and my boss gives me a big thumbs-up, I'm full of pride, but it quickly drowns in the fogginess as I leave the room and return to my desk.

The haze abates somewhat on Tuesday, but what little mental capacity frees up is filled with the mind-boggling question of who my mystery man is. My eyes halt on every man I see to assess whether he seems like the type who'd have the balls to drug me, kidnap me, and claim me as his, then leave me out in the cold alone. Everyone looks benign, though, and my head spins as I stare blankly at all the harmless faces.

The only thing that can get my mind at ease is writing dirty stories. I keep jumping back to the document with my story even as I try to get some real work done, and I end up with one new full story by noon. I don't go back to reread, though, afraid to face the depravities my head has conjured. My old stories are nothing compared to this new level of filth.

Part of me is scared whoever kidnapped me will find my new stories and read them. I'm often about to delete them all from my computer to be safe, but I just can't go through with it. Part of me wants him to find them.

I slowly go crazy, trying to solve the mystery of who took me. Whenever I catch sight of someone in a suit, I whip my head around to get a better look, and whenever I hear a deep voice, I halt in my tracks to listen for that slight note of roughness. But I never hear that rough edge, and the men I see are either too short, have too long hair, too thin fingers, or something else.

Once, I do see someone who has the right height, broad build, and clean-shaven jaw. I end up following him around for the better part of two hours, bringing my laptop to work close by him, and eating lunch in the cafeteria when he does. I've become a full-blown stalker. But when our eyes finally meet, everything shatters to the ground. His gaze is too fleeting. Too vague. There's no hint of the devastating power that filled the very air around the man who commanded my body and my mind so deeply that he took me from being an unwilling victim to willingly submitting to every dirty thing he subjected me to.

When I go into the kitchen on Wednesday morning, the new COO, Matthew Harrington, is there, making coffee. I'm always a bit puzzled when bumping into him here. Our coffee machine can't possibly be better than whatever fancy apparatus they must have up on the executive floor.

As usual, I give a polite, "Hi," and he simply lifts his gaze and smiles in return. I lower my eyes, just for a second. I don't know why, but something about him always prompts me to do so. Maybe it's his very disarming smile—dimples, crinkles at the corners of his eyes, and all. Or maybe it's the directness of his gaze. It radiates authority the same way his tall and proud posture does. But it's not in an arrogant manner as with many of the other men in high positions here. There's this quiet kind of command to him like he doesn't have to make an effort or force it. It comes quite naturally to him. Even as he oozes power, there's this calm confidence to him as he stands there, doing something as simple as making coffee—or tea, I notice with a small frown.

Realizing I'm staring, I quickly turn to open the cupboard where I keep my vanilla chai tea. I'm about to grab the box when an elbow nudges me. I look down to find Matthew placing a cup of tea in front of me on the counter. "Here you go, Sarah," he says.

I turn my head to thank him, but my words falter when he gives my arm a squeeze that somehow seems reassuring.

And then he's gone.

I stare down at my arm like he just burned me. Little sparks of electricity crackle in my skin where he touched me—like I know that touch.

I turn and look after him. *Could it be him?* He's tall with broad shoulders and a fit body, just like the man who held me close that night—after he'd fucked me and stuffed every hole in my body.

Shuddering, I push the memory away. It can't be him. He looks way too nice to do such a thing, and his voice is different. It has no hint of roughness and is not as deep. And his jaw is covered in a short stubble—always is. I breathe a heavy sigh. My need for intimacy is just raging so much that any touch will make my skin come alive.

I stare into the mug and dip the tea bag in and out of the water a few times before I notice the label. Vanilla Chai. My favorite. I wonder if that's part of being a good boss, knowing his employee's drink of choice. I shake my head. Surely, it isn't.

Lifting my gaze, I look through the door, into the office. My desk is right there in my line of sight. It has never bothered me, working in the open like that, but today I wish I could have a desk tucked into a corner where no one would notice me.

Rosa is leaning against my desk, chatting with Marie. Usually, I'd go over there to get the newest office gossip, but I'm in no mood today, so I remain in the kitchen, drinking my tea, until Rosa leaves.

When I return to my desk and check my email, I frown at a request from one of the secretaries on the executive floor, asking me to audit some documents in the filing room on the eighth floor.

"What is it?" Marie asks.

"Sadie wants me to go audit some old documents."

"Why?"

"I have no idea." I scroll down to read further details and find out that it's a huge amount of documents I have to go through. "Are you kidding me? It's gonna take hours."

"Can she do that? I mean, that's not really your job, is it?"

"No," I exclaim, staring at the screen like this stupid request will go away if only I stare hard enough. "And listen to this, she says I may spend an hour a day and draw it out over a few weeks since it's not a pressing matter. *And* she wants me to start today. Then she has the audacity to end by saying her boss very much appreciates my help on this." I flop back in my chair. "Seriously, this is way below my pay grade."

"What are you gonna do? Go talk to her?"

I tap my pen against the desk as I stare to the side, considering this absurd request that apparently comes from higher-up. After a moment of thought, it occurs to me that this might not be so bad, after all. The filing room is in an isolated part of the eighth floor where no one ever goes. It could serve as a welcome escape from the constant bustle of people always eager to chit-chat up here.

Finally, I turn back to Marie. "No. No need to waste my time on that too. It's just an hour a day."

Marie frowns, knowing as well as I do that an hour a day in our busy schedules is a lot. But I get up before she can tell me this, suddenly badly needing to get out of here.

* * *

Pitch-black darkness greets me as I open the door to the filing room. My heart starts pounding, and I almost want to rush back and take Marie's suggestion as I wait for the fluorescents to come on. I breathe a relieved sigh as bright light floods the space, but an eerie feeling remains as I enter and close the door behind me. I might need the seclusion, but it's a bit like finding seclusion in an old mansion with creaky stairs and the wind whistling through the cracks.

Pushing the irrational unease aside, I make my way through the room, past the many tall bookcases teeming with boxes and binders. Of course, the documents I'm looking for are at the very back, where someone could easily corner me and have their way with me.

I shut my eyes and breathe a leveling sigh. Since Friday night, it's been a constant battle to hold paranoid thoughts like this one at bay.

Scanning the many labels in front of me, I search for the first box. I'm about to reach for it when the lights go off. Pitch-black darkness envelops me, and my heavy breaths fill the silence as my chest constricts. I clutch a shelf as the creak of the door resounds through the dead space. A sliver of light softens the darkness, but it's gone in a second as the door closes again.

Holding my breath, I listen for signs of life. *Click, click, click.* The sound of male shoes approaches.

"Hello?" I call out. "Who's there?" With my free hand, I fumble along the wall to search for a switch. I almost slump in relief when I find one and flick it. But nothing happens. Blackness remains, and the steps keep approaching, now dangerously close.

The clicking stops, and my mind thrusts cruel scenarios upon me that have me clutching the shelf tighter and the air in my lungs becoming scarce.

"Who is it?" I try. "Seriously, it's not funny. Please turn the lights back on."

Click, click, click.

His presence looms right in front of me, and I press myself back into the corner as my mind screams at me to run. But there's no place to go. I'm trapped. Helpless in the darkness once again.

I want to scream as fingers graze my chest, but the sound dies in a gasp as hands grab me and pull me up against a strong body.

"No, no, no," I start, pushing at a way too hard chest. "Let me go."

"Shh," he soothes and cups the back of my head, trailing his other hand down my spine. "You're safe."

I freeze. That slight edge or roughness is there, in his words. *It's him.* My hands quiver as I move them slightly, feeling the familiar width of his chest and the gentle ripple of muscles beneath. "It's really you?"

"It's me," he confirms.

Those words are my undoing. Emotions crash through my system—fast and violently. I've barely been holding myself up for the last few days, constantly about to crumble under the loneliness and confusion that have wreaked havoc on me. Now I don't have to do it by myself anymore, and I collapse against him as my knees finally give in under the pressure.

With an arm around my waist, he easily

catches me and lowers us both to the floor, where he leans against the wall with me curled up between his legs.

"You look awfully lost, pretty girl." He brushes his knuckles over my cheek. "Like a droopy little flower."

"I feel lost." I swallow the lump in my throat and close my eyes to hold in the stinging tears. I want to say more but hesitate, afraid it will burst the dam, yet the need to get the words out is too strong. "I need you," I end up blurting.

A tear spills from my eye, and I hold my breath as it slides toward his hand where it's still stroking. I tense up as it touches his skin, and time seems to stop as he reaches up to feel the side of my eye just as another tear drips free.

"You didn't go to the police," he says in a soft voice.

I shake my head and breathe a shuddery sigh. "How could I?"

"You need me," he repeats, affirming the words like they're all the confirmation he needs. "You're mine now." He wraps an arm around my waist and pulls me close, and that's when the tears start falling in earnest. I don't weep or sob; it's just tears and ragged breaths as I shake against him, clutching the lapels of his suit jacket as if my life depended on it.

I don't know how long we sit here in silence, him stroking me tenderly and me clinging to him, but it's a long time. Somewhere along the way, the desperate energy fades, and I relax against him, soaking up his warmth and strength as I curl up against his chest and sink into quiet restfulness.

"I have to get back to work," he finally says, bursting the bubble.

"Me too." I straighten and hug my arms awkwardly around my waist. Remembering all the files I have to audit, I release a heavy sigh and mutter, "Too much work." There's no way I'll be going home on time today.

"You don't have to audit those files." He finds my arms through the darkness and helps me to my feet. "But I need you to be here at the same time for the rest of the week, okay?"

I'm about to ask a bunch of questions, but the words die on my tongue as he presses the pad of his thumb to my lips and strokes back and forth. His touch is like a kiss, and it makes me crave his lips. Slowly, I lean up on my tiptoes, my hands moving up his chest. The moment I reach the edges of his shirt, he snaps his hands around my wrists.

"Uh, uh," he scolds and lowers my hands back to his chest. Then he wraps his arms around me, pulling me close to him. His grip slowly tightens, and a sort of primal energy buzzes in the air as he slides one hand up my back to wrap it around my neck.

"You're mine," he growls, yanking me so close

my lungs constrict. "Remember that, or there'll be consequences."

My response is a slight whimper. I can't get anything else out through my compressed chest, and my mind can't seem to form any words.

"I'm going to leave now. Once I'm gone, I want you to sit back down and slide your fingers into your pants and feel your sweet little pussy. Take your time. Start by stroking your lips gently, then move on to your clit, and finally shove two fingers inside. Just as those inner walls start to contract and your toes begin to curl, I want you to thank me. Once those words have passed your lips, you may come. Then take a moment to calm down, lick your fingers clean, and go up and finish for the day."

"I can't—" I don't get to finish my protest about masturbating at work before he cuts me off with a sharp tone.

"Are we clear?"

"Yes," I blurt in a breathy voice.

"Good girl." He pats my cheek and rewards me with a soft kiss on top of my head. Then he's gone. The clicking of shoes rings out through the space, the door opens and closes, and I'm once again alone.

A minute later, the lights come back on, and I find I almost miss the darkness. Or maybe it's him I'm missing—so much I almost can't bear it.

Anxiety and longing twist together in my

chest. The emotions are almost about to get the better of me, and I think I won't be able to fend off the tears this time, but when I sink down against the wall and slip my hands into my wet panties, another urge takes precedence. I rub myself to a staggering orgasm that has me slapping my hand over my mouth to stop myself from screaming out loud.

CHAPTER 9

I spend an hour in the filing room with him on both Thursday and Friday. Each day, he starts by cuffing my hands behind my back before he pulls me into a tight hug. When I ask him about the restriction, he simply says he doesn't want my hands to roam freely. I remember how he stopped me when I tried to touch his face and how he didn't kiss me, and I wonder if that's why he uses the cuffs.

The question dissipates from my mind when he slips his fingers into my panties. He sinks to the floor with me in his arms, where he takes his sweet time stroking my folds before he shoves his fingers inside me. He gives me two orgasms like that, then holds me close as I shudder in his arms, coming down from the high.

It's a good thing we're here late in the day because my head is all in a daze when I return to the office—only now, a comfortable, cloudy daze instead of the heavy one that dragged me down at the start of the week.

Now, instead of coming into work with slouched shoulders and head hanging low, I'm bright and bubbly, full of anticipation as I go about my day, waiting for when it's time to go to the filing room.

Friday afternoon, I stay in the filing room after the lights have come back on, too ruffled by the heady intimacy to return to the office straight away. Knowing I might feel this way, I brought my laptop, and I stay on the floor, working for an hour before I finally feel settled enough to go back and face the world.

The office is quiet when I return. I sense the calmness already when I step out of the elevator despite the glass walls separating the large offices from the lobby. Most people have gone home early, and only a few remain by their computers, probably hurrying to finish whatever they're doing so they, too, can start their weekends.

When I step up to the glass door, I halt as Matthew approaches from the inside. He's probably here to grab his last cup of coffee for the day—I really have to ask him what's so special about our coffee that he always comes down here. The sight of a tall man in a suit still has this startling effect on me, and my mind immediately starts whirring, wondering, and assessing.

He flashes me a disarming smile as he opens the door and holds it for me. "Have a nice weekend," he says in a smooth, velvety voice.

I step inside and spin on my heel, gazing after him through the glass as he walks to the elevator. *That voice.* It's him. It has to be. His voice may lack the roughness and depth, but it has that same steady quality that lulled me into peaceful tranquility in the darkness of the filing room.

Or maybe I'm imagining things because I need to find out. Our encounter was way too brief for me to be sure. God, my head is a mess.

Castigating myself mentally, I make my way through the quiet office to my desk at the back. Once again, I stop abruptly. This time it's because of a small black box and an envelope sitting before my keyboard. My heart starts palpitating, and I gaze up, through the room and to the lobby where Matthew just stepped into the elevator. Did he just leave this here?

I pick up the envelope while my eyes keep flickering back and forth between the white paper and the elevator. Then I close my eyes and force my breathing to slow down and my head to do the same. It just might be a coincidence. Anyone could have been here during the time I spent alone in the filing room.

Shaking my head at myself, I turn my attention to the envelope and open it. A piece of thick, white paper has two lines scribbled at the center in neat penmanship.

I've read one of your new stories. If you're ready to own up to your desires, use the contents of the black box and be ready at the following address tonight at eight O'clock.

I flip the paper to find an address scribbled on the back.

I use my phone to search the address and frown when I find it's in the industrial park on the Western outskirts of town. That place will be completely dead tonight.

Gulping back the sudden nervousness in my throat, I lift the black box that looks like something that might contain some expensive jewelry a little bigger than a ring. As if expecting to find a snake or poisonous spider, I lift the lid very slowly, and what I find has my heart beating the same way a dangerous animal would.

A small vial with two black contact lenses rests on the black velvet interior.

My eyes dart up, and I scan the room frantically as a wary feeling skitters down my spine. Almost expecting someone to jump out of a hiding place and assault me, I'm tempted to look under every desk, or rather, bolt. After all the comfort, sweet orgasms, and tender words in the filing room, I've almost forgotten how dangerous this man is. I've forgotten how this all started.

Last Friday, I didn't have a choice, but this time I do.

I know what my choice should be, but I also know this will all end if I don't show up at the secluded address, and I don't know if I can bear that.

With a shake of my head, I rid myself of the thought and stare back up at the elevator, trying to recall all the times I've bumped into Matthew. He seems too friendly—too much scruff, too smooth a voice—to be the man behind all this. Yet everything else fits. His height, his build, his calm yet all-consuming authority. Even the warmth in his smile matches the warmth I've felt in his touch. So maybe he's just good at hiding his primal side?

My heart skips a beat at the thought.

He's always in the kitchen down here where he has a perfect view of my desk. He could have easily been in there, sipping his coffee at lunch while watching me type away as my cheeks went rosy. As if that's not enough, his position in the company might grant him access to the employee's computers. Or maybe he simply knows no one would do anything if they found him breaching into my files.

It has to be him.

Yet I'm not sure of anything as I go home and prepare for the nerve-racking situation I'm about to put myself in. Because really, there's no choice. Whether I want it or not, I'm his. He has branded himself so deeply into me that my own will doesn't matter anymore.

CHAPTER 10

The rain patters gently on the rooftops and roads as I leave my apartment half an hour before eight, and the water wets the asphalt and glitters under the streetlights. Stopping for a moment, I crane my neck to gaze up at the sky. It's easy to forget about the bustling city and the lights surrounding me as I stare at the almost full moon. It's mesmerizing. And ominous. With the stars blinded by the lights of the city and dark clouds covering half the sky, the bright orb stands out like a blaring light on a black canvas. As I keep watching, the city's life slips further and further away from my consciousness until it feels like the moon is sucking me into the sky to wrap me up in darkness.

I shudder as I remember the black contact lenses in my bag, which will soon do just that.

Shaking off the thought, I clutch my shoulder bag and head for my car. It takes me a little over twenty minutes to reach my destination, and I'm about to turn around and return to the bustling city several times as I drive through the empty industry park and find the right address in the middle of it all.

This place is as secluded as can be. Even a dark forest has birds, bugs, and bright stars. Here, everything is *dead.* I can barely even hear any traffic. Only the artificial lights lend the place some sense of life, but really, they're deceptive—a means to scare off unwelcome intruders. Except, they won't scare off my intruder. He'll come and take me and use me however he pleases. This is the only thing I'm sure of.

I close my eyes and lean my head back into the seat as I try to calm my frantic breathing. The rain taps on the roof of my car like a bad omen of what's to come. *It's just gentle rain,* I remind myself and take myself back to a memory of going camping with my dad as a child. The rain was soothing back then, lulling me to sleep. I let it calm me now too and manage to get my breathing under control. Then I straighten and reach inside my pocket for the vial with the contacts.

A hundred different scenarios—one more scary than the other—whir in my head as I stare at the black lenses. *I shouldn't do this,* my brain screams at me, but it's not my brain controlling me as I take out a lens, lean up to the rearview mirror, and lift my eyelid to put it in.

Fear creeps along my spine the moment half

my sight disappears. I turn my head from side to side, searching for some sign of life or threat out there—to make sure I'm safe once I step outside blind.

It's stupid, really, because I'm anything but safe. I know he's here somewhere or will be shortly, and I wouldn't know it was him even if I saw him. Even a stranger might be less dangerous than him. *Fuck.* Once I put these in, I'm right where he wants me, helpless to the bone.

Even knowing this, I take the second lens out and put it in.

My world descends into darkness, and my breathing and the pattering rain seem to grow louder as I become acutely aware of the sounds around me. I move my hand against the car door until I find the handle, grab it with my clammy hand, and open it. A gush of fresh wind invites me into the unknown open, and I step out on quivering legs and shut the door to the safety of my car.

I gulp as I remain there for a moment, a hand on my car, just listening.

Nothing.

The rain trickles down on my head, wetting my hair with tiny droplets as I release my car and take a step toward the entrance of the building that holds the number scribbled on the paper. I have no idea whether he'll bring me inside, have his way with me here in the open, or take me somewhere else, but something tells me he doesn't want me to remain by my car like a coward ready to flee.

I take five more steps, and anxiety crawls along my spine as I sense the open space surrounding me on all sides—nothing to grab or seek safety by.

I move my head, trying to catch any sounds, but everything remains dead. The anxiety turns into a pulsing fear that thrums in my chest with the urge to do something—anything. I turn around repeatedly, and the fear pounds even harder as I lose all sense of direction.

I shouldn't be here, is all I can think as my fingers twitch with the urge to take out the contacts. But another part of me—the part that craves his touch with mighty desire—keeps me still, frozen in time, frozen in place. There, I wait for two, five, maybe ten minutes.

Nothing happens—until it does.

Footsteps are a vague sound in the distance. At first, I'm not sure they're even there, but as they grow louder, I become certain. Someone is here, and they're closing in.

Click, click, click, click.

I spin around again, trying to gauge where they're coming from.

Click, click, click, click.

The sound echoes off the buildings, messing with my sense of direction and distance.

Click, click, click, click.

The sound grows louder, and then I sense it. A strong presence close by.

I turn to face the direction they're coming from even as I start backing up. I'm no longer thinking. It's pure instinct. Stupid, stupid instinct. I should take out the lenses and run like hell, I vaguely realize, but I'm caught in this slow retreat—trapped by my panicked mind.

The steps become faster as if he senses my urge to flee. I spin around and pick up my pace, waving my hands blindly in front of me to avert a collision.

"No, no, no," I whimper. What if it's not him? What if it's some creep who has spotted me and wants to prey on my vulnerability? And what if it *is* him?

Finally, my brain kicks in, and I shoot a hand up to remove the contacts. But my hands are shaky, my coordination messy.

Click, click, click, click.

The steps are right behind me now.

"No, no, no!" I cry, setting off in a shuffling half-run, not caring if I slam into something. I just need to get away.

Instead of slamming into something in front of me, I slam into a hard chest behind me as a hand clamps over my mouth.

"You're not going anywhere," a deep voice says with a cruel snarl that sounds like *him*, but I can't be sure.

I writhe against him, but he simply locks the other arm around my waist, effectively trapping my arms at my sides.

"You're mine," he growls in a familiar voice that sets my blood running cold even as it grounds me through the panicked chaos. "Mine to use and abuse however I like until the break of dawn."

This time, I'm sure it's him. It's his voice, his touch, and his words. The realization is as relieving as it is distressing as the memory of him raping me crashes against the memory of him holding me tenderly.

He drags me backward, and I kick my heels into the ground, trying to find some kind of purchase or maybe still trying to wrest free.

I shouldn't have come, is all I can think as he shoves me to the ground. My knees scrape against harsh concrete, ripping my pantyhose and my skin. Grabbing me by the hair, he lowers me to lie face-down on the ground. I try to push up as my face connects with cold, wet asphalt, but I'm so disoriented I barely lift my chest before he's on top of me, pinning me to the cold ground.

Then everything changes in a charged moment of tender intimacy as he gently cocoons me with his body and presses a soft kiss to my cheek. My heart swells at the warm feeling of his lips—his smooth, clean-shaved skin—and I forget about the cold ground as he lifts my head back to capture my lips in an achingly tender kiss. I've ached for those lips since he denied me a kiss in the filing room on Wednesday—I've ached for those lips since our last kiss on Friday.

He hums like he's thinking the same thing, and I melt into his warm body, wanting nothing more than to give in to his touch—his dominance.

That is until he shatters all sense of safety with a single sentence. "Is it rape if the victim willingly showed up?"

ALSO BY ELLA JACOBS
Excerpt from In His Cage

A Dark Abduction Romance

"Keep walking," a deep voice commands, all too calmly.

I want to turn my head—see who's got the nerve to grab me and press a knife to my back in broad daylight. But I can't. Fear has me paralyzed, unable to think or act. My legs are the only thing working, and only because they have to.

All I can see from the corner of my eye is his left side—white and black clothes, tall and broad frame. He's so tall his face is hidden way above my head where I don't dare cast my eyes up. His fingers are large enough to encompass my upper arm in an unbreakable grip. It's not forceful, but the potential strength is palpable. He could easily snap my bones.

Icy shivers skate down my skin, and my legs quiver, threatening to give in. But fear is not the only thing churning in my stomach. There's this feeling of powerlessness that tugs at something deep inside me—some magnetic pull, against all rationality, that flutters and sends heat coursing through my veins.

It's his presence. It looms over me like a great building casting its shadow over several blocks, calm and powerful. Commanding in a most masculine way that speaks to my feminine soul and keeps my heart from speeding too fast. It's like the unwavering stability steadies me through the fear that wreaks havoc on my insides.

Fuck. I must be sick. There's nothing alluring about a stranger who presses a knife to my back, possibly kidnapping me.

The blood drains from my face and bile rises in my throat.

Is that what's happening? He's kidnapping me?

I'm going to be sick at any moment. The telltale stomach cramps have already set in.

"That's it," the man says, voice slow and deep—praising? "Keep going. Straight ahead." It's almost like he senses the oncoming nausea. Like he's trying to reduce the immediate threat with soothing words.

It's ridiculous. I know there's nothing safe about those words. They're a twisted illusion.

Yet my stomach settles.

He guides me through the exit and onto the raised parking lot on a large platform. I hear a train pull in below us, screeching on the tracks as it comes to a halt. A woman walks past us with hastened steps—maybe to catch said train—and she doesn't even spare us a glance.

I want to reach out and tug at her, scream for help. But I don't dare. And as the man behind me moves us across the platform, toward the stairs at the corner, help slips out of reach.

I know what's down there beneath the long set of stairs.

Nothing.

The stairs lead to the secluded side of the station, where people only come when the parking space up here is full. And it sure isn't today.

The shaking spreads through my body, and I start staggering.

I abruptly halt at the edge of the stairs and stare down the immense amount of steps. "I can't," I croak. Somehow, it seems worse falling down all those steps than being dragged away by this stranger. "I'll fall."

"*Dershu tebya.* I won't let you fall." As if to prove his point, he tightens his grip on my arm.

It's like déjà vu—the steadying hand and deep voice.

That's when it hits me. The man on the train. White and black. His suit.

I turn my head and stare straight up into chilly blue eyes. Cold as a block of ice, yet warm with the promise he just made. It doesn't make sense—not the dichotomy in his eyes, not the kidnapping.

I'm so stunned my fear fades for a moment,

making my feet move on autopilot as he nudges me.

Fresh notes of citrus and something masculine waft past my nose as I move my feet onto the first step, and I inadvertently inhale a deep whiff of the intoxicating scent. *His scent.*

"One step at a time. I'll catch you if you fall."

He must be mocking me for my unsteady feet—or maybe my fall on the platform earlier. But I find no ridicule in his words. They are smooth and warm. Tender even. Maybe he actually means it?

It can't be. How can someone be tender while holding a knife to my back?

My brain fogs over with all the questions and contradictions. Yet somehow, I manage to zero in on the task of placing one foot on each step—a task that seems more like climbing a mountain than a simple everyday action.

I barely notice that the sharp tip at my back disappears and a flat palm presses against my waist instead. Supporting me?

It takes forever to descend those stairs, and when I finally have both feet back on solid ground, it takes me a moment to gather my thoughts. Before I can think of running, the knife is back against my skin. The man leads me to the dusty single parking lot in front of the rails, where a single large SUV is parked in the shadow of the platform.

My skin stings beneath the tip of the knife, but

the pain is nothing compared to the one bearing down on my chest. I can barely breathe through it, and my inhales become more and more ragged as we approach the car.

The faint noise of traffic hums in the distance, but it's so low I barely notice it. My wheezing breath and the crunch of shoes on gravel seem to be the only sounds around us.

Stopping by the SUV, the man opens the back door, and I see the silhouette of another man in the driver's seat. The driver is large and bulky, like one of those men you see pulling a truck on TV.

Heavy blocks of ice settle in my stomach. I can't get into that car. When I'm in, there's no out. I know it like I know sunsets leave darkness, heavy clouds bring rain. And like the weather, I see no stopping this. Yet my mind scrambles to work something out.

Should I fight? Scream? Is it worth risking a knife in my back?

Indecision pounds in my head, dragging on in a single second that seems to last forever.

Then the last question becomes void as the knife hits the ground with a metallic sound. The sharp tip is gone, and I know what I have to do.

There's no way I'm getting into that car.

With a forceful yank of my arm, I open my mouth to scream. But I'm too slow. Before the shrill sound can ring out into the open space, a large hand clamps over my mouth.

"Don't even think about it." The words are a low snarl, and for a moment, I think it's someone else—maybe the man in the car who has come out. It can't be the same voice as the one crooning in my ear moments ago. "The knife was just a means to keep you calm. But down here, I'm not beyond using force."

It's the same man. The citrusy scent from before wafts past my nose again, and the other man is still in the driver's seat. There's no one else here. The man snarling in my ear is the same one who pressed a supportive hand against my waist and promised he wouldn't let me fall.

Maintaining the punishing grip on my bicep, he removes his palm from my mouth, and what little courage I had gathered fades fast.

There's a rustle of clothes—a hand digging into a pocket. The seconds stretch on, and I don't understand why he doesn't shove me into the vehicle.

Something new drops to the ground. Plastic? I glance down, and yes, there on the gravel lies a small, oblong plastic cap, and somehow, that lid is more terrifying than the knife beside it.

The man pulls down my arm, stretching my shoulder. And then I feel it. The most terrifying thing of all. A small prick, then an aching pressure as liquid seeps into my muscle.

I whimper—a small, weak sound. My body slackens as my strength seeps out with frightening speed. My limbs go numb, and my knees give in. I collapse.

As the man promised, he catches me. Strong arms easily support my weight, holding me against a hard chest.

Using my last sliver of strength, I crane my neck and gaze up into a set of blue eyes boring into my very soul. I don't recognize the features around them, but I recognize the intensity of those eyes.

It *is* him. Aleksandr Pletnev.

"It's you..." My voice fades before I can say more.

"You're mine now." His lips tip up into a wide, charming smile—the smile I so badly wanted on the train. Now, he finally aims it at me, and it's the most terrifying thing I've ever seen.

The last thing I see before my world goes black.

ABOUT ELLA JACOBS

Ella Jacobs writes BDSM and dark romance. She loves exploring the emotional sides to Dom/sub relationships and subjecting her heroines to overbearing men with gray morals.

Besides writing, Ella loves music. It inspires her to write, and when her characters are messing with her head, she sits down at the piano and plays Chopin and Liszt to regain her sanity.

Ella lives her own age gap romance with a stern, loving Dominant, who is always ready for some character analysis and rarely gets jealous when she falls in love with her fictive men.

You can read more about her own experiences with the BDSM lifestyle on her website.

www.ellajacobs.com

Printed in Dunstable, United Kingdom

72682040R00063